For Elodie and her Grandad,
who quietly made the world a wonderful place to be.

– Z. A.

To Steve and Paul, who love trees more than
anyone I know. And to my friend Nita, to whom
I dedicate every single pigeon in this book.

– A. V.

First edition published in 2025 by Flying Eye Books Ltd.
27 Westgate Street, London, E8 3RL.
www.flyingeyebooks.com

Represented by: Authorised Rep Compliance Ltd. Ground Floor,
71 Lower Baggot Street, Dublin, D02 P593, Ireland.
www.arccompliance.com

Text © Zoë Armstrong 2025
Illustrations © Amélie Videlo 2025

Zoë Armstrong and Amélie Videlo have asserted their rights under the Copyright,
Designs and Patents Act, 1988, to be identified as the Author and Illustrator of this Work.

All rights reserved. No part of this publication may be reproduced or transmitted in any form
or by any means, electronic or mechanical, including photocopying, recording or by any
information and storage retrieval system, without prior written consent from the publisher.

No part of this book may be used or reproduced in any manner for the purpose of training
artificial intelligence technologies or systems. Flying Eye Books Ltd expressly reserves
The Great Oak Tree from the text and data mining exception, in accordance with
Article 4 of European Parliament Directive (EU) 2019/790.

Edited by Christina Webb
Designed by Lilly Gottwald

Consultant: The Tree Council

1 3 5 7 9 10 8 6 4 2

UK ISBN: 978-1-83874-217-1
US ISBN: 978-1-83874-963-7

Printed in Latvia on FSC® certified paper.

Zoë Armstrong   Amélie Videlo

THE GREAT OAK TREE

Flying Eye Books

There was a great oak tree at the edge of the woods.

It was always there. The sun shone on the tree, the winds rustled its leaves and the rains pitter pattered through its branches.

And the tree stood.

All around the tree was the bustle of activity.

Squirrels scampered up its craggy trunk. Birds made their nests in the tree's wide canopy. Flowers sprang up and turned their faces towards the milky sunshine.

A little blackbird called out rudely to the tree, "Look how busy we all are, doing important things. Why do *you* never move, Tree?"

"The tree is busy with important things too," cooed a wise old owl.

The blackbird laughed and said, "But it's been standing there for a hundred years!"

"Four hundred, actually," said the owl.

The tree drank deeply from the ground, too busy for all this talk.

It was moving syrupy sap up from its roots, up through its trunk and out along its branches to feed the little leaves that were beginning to unfurl.

Pollen drifted into the air from strings of yellow flowers that dangled from the tree. Squirrels and insects feasted on the flowers, while birds rushed about, bringing food for their chicks.

A bird of prey circled overhead. The little blackbird shrieked and panicked and dashed to the tree for safety.

Summer came.

The tree caught sunlight with its many leaves.

The wise old owl told the blackbird how the tree used the sunshine to make food, so it could grow.

And how the tree took carbon from the air and breathed out oxygen, which gave life to all the different creatures.

A hot haze enveloped the woods.

The sound of crickets filled the air,
a cat stretched out in the shade
and acorns grew in little woody cups.

But the tree was under attack! Earwigs, caterpillars, weevils and mites nibbled its leaves and gnawed its branches.

Gall wasp larvae grew inside some of the acorns, turning them knobbly and strange.

"Help! Help!" shrieked the little blackbird. "The tree is being eaten alive!"

The wise old owl told the little blackbird how the tree was busy defending itself.

"It has tough bark to protect its trunk and branches; It makes bitter chemicals so its leaves will not taste good."

"But we must help the tree!" cried the little blackbird. "We must eat those insects before they eat our friend!"

The owl chuckled and said, yes, they would try.

"The spiders and bats will help too," said the owl.

The sun sank lower in the sky and the days grew shorter. Autumn was here.

The tree pulled the green from its leaves and turned it into food to store for winter.

A wild wind whipped about the tree, snatching leaves from its branches and rattling acorns to the ground.

The little blackbird clung to the tree for shelter with the other birds.

Fading flowers fell over in the wind, but the tree stood tall. Its roots were strong like an anchor and wide like a fan.

All was calm.

Clouds came down and settled like a damp lid over the woods.

An acorn landed with a soft thud on the head of a passing boar. The boar gobbled the acorn and trotted away.

The wise old owl told the little blackbird how the acorn held a seed, and that the seed was the very beginning of a new tree.

"But now the seed is inside the boar!" said the little blackbird, alarmed.

The owl chuckled and said the seed would surely exit the boar later, and perhaps grow somewhere new.

The little blackbird laughed at the funny wonder of it all.

"Help!" cried the little blackbird. "The tree is naked! It will freeze!"

"Don't worry," said the wise old owl. "Its bark is like a blanket for keeping out the cold."

The little blackbird listened as the owl told him how the tree was preparing for the dark months ahead.

"Its leaves are too tender to survive the chill," said the owl. "And they are no use for catching light under the weak winter sun."

The air grew sharper.

Spiders huddled into the tree's cracks and crevices for warmth, a bat folded itself away inside a woody hole. A winter moth crawled up the tree to lay her eggs.

Inside, the tree was working hard to survive.

The wise old owl told the little blackbird how the tree was pulling water out of its cells to leave behind a rich, sugary liquid that would keep the tree from freezing.

Snow fell and muffled the woods with its softness. The boughs of the tree creaked, but they were strong and they cradled the heavy load.

A tangle of mistletoe decorated the tree with berries. The little blackbird peeked out of a cosy hollow.

A robin sang, the owl watched and the tree slept.

One day, the sun peeped over the top of the tree, and the woods began to thaw.

"Wake up, Tree! Wake up!" cried a little woodpecker, drumming her beak against the bark.

"Shh," said the blackbird, gently – he wasn't so little anymore. "The tree is doing important things."

And he told the little woodpecker all about his friend the great oak tree, who was quietly very busy making the world a wonderful place to be.